Wave Dancer™ Is Missing!

by M.J. Carr
Illustrated by Christine Finn

SCHOLASTIC INC.

New York Toronto London Auckland Sydney

ISBN 0-590-46604-6

Copyright © 1993 Playskool, Inc.
All rights reserved. Published by Scholastic Inc.,
by arrangement with Playskool, Inc., 1027 Newport Avenue, Pawtucket, RI 02862.
MY PRETTY MERMAID, WAVE DANCER, and SEA SPLASHER
are trademarks of Playskool, Inc.

12 11 10 9 8 7 6 5 4 3   3 4 5 6 7 8/9

Printed in the U.S.A.   24

First Scholastic printing, May 1993

Deep under the sea, past the coral reefs, past the sunken galleons, there lived a school of mermaids. All of the mermaids in the school were good swimmers. Some were swift and some were best at diving, but one was particularly graceful. When she moved through the water, it looked as if she were dancing. Her name was Wave Dancer™.

This time each year, when the summer sun began to warm the water, the school had a contest — a scavenger hunt. For this contest the mermaids' swimming skills had to be extra sharp. So they practiced every spare moment.

It was Wave Dancer's first year at the school and she wasn't sure she was ready to compete. She was much better at dancing. She could twist and turn, hula and jig.

The morning of the contest, the school's head-mermaid, MerMadame, called all the young mermaids together. "Now, you all know that mermaids must swim fast, swim far, and find their way through the depths of the ocean," she said. "Today you will need to do all three."

MerMadame pulled out a long, broad piece of driftwood. On it was a list of things to look for in the scavenger hunt. MerMadame read the list aloud: "Three giant clamshells, two bright pink conch shells, a foot-long piece of giant kelp seaweed, three sunken coins, and a fan-shaped coral.

The first team to find and bring back all of these things will be the winner," said MerMadame.

MerMadame divided up the young mermaids. Sea Splasher™ was captain of Wave Dancer's team. The mermaids on the team huddled around her. Sea Splasher had a plan.

"We'll split up," she told her friends. "Each of us will swim off to find one of the things on the list. That way we'll be sure to be the first team back."

Sea Splasher chose Wave Dancer to look for the sunken coins. Wave Dancer was floating off, dancing, as if she heard music. The others heard no such thing.

"Hmm," said Sea Splasher. "We'd better send Dolph with her. He'll be sure to keep her on course." Sea Splasher knew she could depend on Dolph. Dolph was MerMadame's trusted assistant.

Wave Dancer was happy to hear that they would travel together. "Let's go, Dolph!" she said smiling. And so, Dolph swam off with Wave Dancer in her search for the sunken coins.

Soon they came upon a shaft of sunlight streaming through the blue water. Wave Dancer began dancing up through the shimmering beam of light.

"Wave Dancer! This way!" Dolph called. "Sunken coins are at the *bottom* of the ocean!

But Wave Dancer continued to drift upwards.

"Wave Dancer!" Dolph cried from below. "Swim toward the *floor* of the ocean. It's *sunken* coins we want!"

But Wave Dancer was not listening. She drifted higher still, toward the surface — toward danger!

As she danced dreamily, floating upwards, Wave Dancer suddenly felt something drop around her. She snapped out of her daze.

"What's that?" she cried. It was a fishing net! She was caught! Wave Dancer tore at the net, struggling to get free.

Dolph sped toward her. He tried to chew through
the rope, but it was too strong. He knew he would have to
get help.

In the net were lots of fish. All of them were frightened, flopping and flipping. Wave Dancer felt the net start to lift and strain. It was being pulled out of the water! Wave Dancer burrowed to the bottom as quickly as she could.

The net was dropped on the deck of a large fishing boat. Fishermen crowded around, sorting through the fish. They threw the smallest ones back into the water. At the bottom of the pile was Wave Dancer, trembling, frightened. "Hey, mates!" cried one of the fishermen. "Will you look what we have here!"

The fishermen filled a barrel with salt water and plunged
Wave Dancer in. "We'll bring her to land," one said. "And a
fine price she'll fetch for us."

As the ship rocked back and forth, Wave Dancer looked out across the surface of the ocean. The sun was blindingly bright on the water. Wave Dancer thought she saw a head or two bob above the waves. It looked like Sea Splasher! And Dolph! "It must be the sun playing tricks on my eyes," she murmured to herself.

Night fell. One by one the fishermen went below to go to sleep. Wave Dancer was left alone in the barrel at one end of the ship. Quietly a young boy crept up to get a closer look at her. Now's my chance, she thought.

"I don't belong here," Wave Dancer cried to the boy. "I belong in the sea. Please set me free!" But the boy did not understand the language of mermaids. He didn't even know she was speaking to him. He stared at her strangely. Then he took out his hornpipe and began to play.

As the melody drifted in the still night air, Wave Dancer
began to dance. The boy kept playing, and watched her,
spellbound.

When he finished his song, he put down the hornpipe. He looked long and hard at Wave Dancer. She looked back at him, her eyes pleading. "You don't belong on land," the boy whispered. "You belong in the water where you can be free to dance through the waves."

He looked around to make sure that no one was watching. Then he dragged the barrel to the edge of the ship and tipped Wave Dancer back into the sea.

As Wave Dancer crashed through the surface of the water, she felt a ring of arms catch her. She looked around. "Sea Splasher! Dolph!" she cried. Her team had followed her to the ship! She *had* seen them after all!

As Wave Dancer rested from her night above water,
Sea Splasher stayed close to her side.

"I guess we didn't win the contest," said Wave Dancer.

Sea Splasher shook her head. "No," she answered.
"We came in last."

Just then, MerMadame swam up to them. "You may have come in last," she said, "but in their search for you, all the mermaids on your team showed great bravery and courage." She gave each of the mermaids a special ribbon. "Next year, we've decided to have a different kind of contest."

"For bravery and courage?" asked Sea Splasher.

"No," said MerMadame. She winked at Wave Dancer. "It will be for dancing."